W9-APL-180

Dear Parent:
Your child's love of reading starts here!

Every child learns to read in a different way and at his or her own speed. You can help your young reader improve and become more confident by encouraging his or her own interests and abilities. You can also guide your child's spiritual development by reading stories with biblical values and Bible stories, like I Can Read! books published by Zonderkidz. From books your child reads with you to the first books he or she reads alone, there are I Can Read! books for every stage of reading:

SHARED READING
Basic language, word repetition, and whimsical illustrations, ideal for sharing with your emergent reader.

BEGINNING READING
Short sentences, familiar words, and simple concepts for children eager to read on their own.

READING WITH HELP
Engaging stories, longer sentences, and language play for developing readers.

READING ALONE
Complex plots, challenging vocabulary, and high-interest topics for the independent reader.

ADVANCED READING
Short paragraphs, chapters, and exciting themes for the perfect bridge to chapter books.

I Can Read! books have introduced children to the joy of reading since 1957. Featuring award-winning authors and illustrators and a fabulous cast of beloved characters, I Can Read! books set the standard for beginning readers.

A lifetime of discovery begins with the magical words **"I Can Read!"**

Visit www.icanread.com for information on enriching your child's reading experience.
Visit www.zonderkidz.com for more Zonderkidz I Can Read! titles.

"None of you should look out just for your own good. You should also look out for the good of others."
— Philippians 2:4

ZONDERKIDZ

Princess Petunia and the Good Knight
Copyright © 2012 by Big Idea, Inc. VEGGIETALES.® character names, likenesses and other indicia are trademarks of Big Idea, Inc. All rights reserved.

Requests for information should be addressed to:

Zondervan, 5300 Patterson Ave SE, Grand Rapids, Michigan 49530

ISBN 978-0-310-73206-8

All Scripture quotations, unless otherwise indicated, are taken from the Holy Bible, *New International Reader's Version®, NIrV®*. Copyright © 1995, 1996, 1998 by Biblica, Inc.™ Used by permission. All rights reserved worldwide.

Any Internet addresses (websites, blogs, etc.) and telephone numbers in this book are offered as a resource. They are not intended in any way to be or imply an endorsement by Zondervan, nor does Zondervan vouch for the content of these sites and numbers for the life of this book.

All rights reserved. No part of this publication may be reproduced, stored in a retrieval system, or transmitted in any form or by any means—electronic, mechanical, photocopy, recording, or any other—except for brief quotations in printed reviews, without the prior permission of the publisher.

Zonderkidz is a trademark of Zondervan.

Editor: Mary Hassinger
Art direction: Kris Nelson
Cover design: Karen Poth
Interior design: Karen Poth

Printed in China

13 14 15 16 /DSC/ 22 21 20 19 18 17 16 15 14 13 12 11 10 9 8 7 6 5 4 3 2

ZONDERkidz

I Can Read!

BEGINNING READING 1

Princess Petunia and the Good Knight

story by Karen Poth

The Castle of Scone

was a busy place!

Everyone came to see

the Great Pie Games!

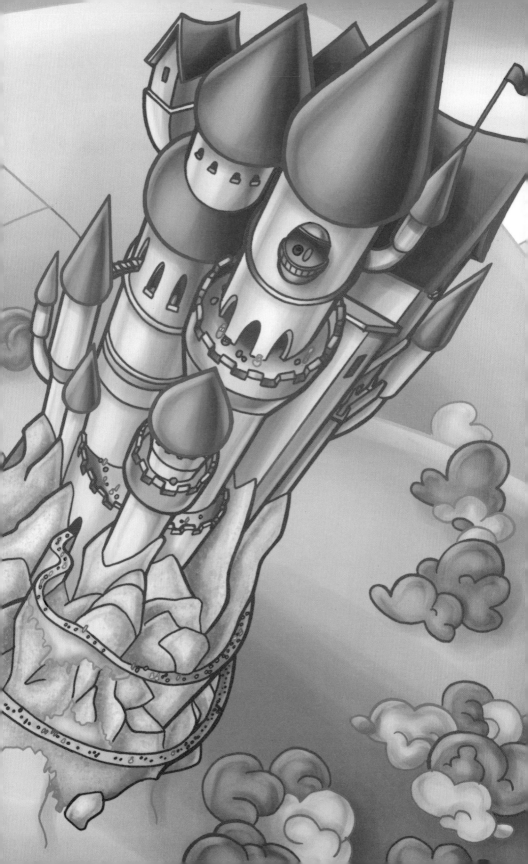

Music played!

The Peas sang!

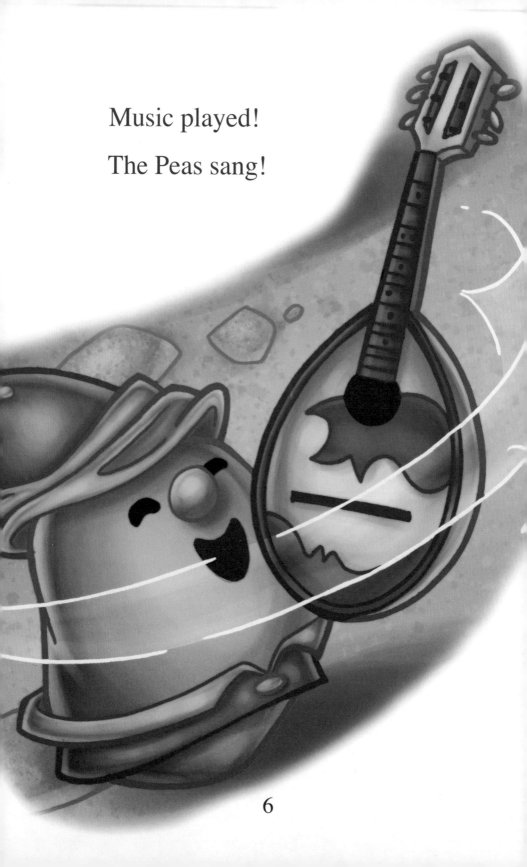

All the Veggies were happy!
They waited for the games
to start.

Princess Petunia looked
down at the field.
She saw a table piled
with fresh, sticky pies.
There were many brave men
waiting to play!

As the pie games began,

pies flew everywhere.

Bump in the Knight won!

"I am the greatest!" he said.

He was bragging.

He was not a very nice knight.

The crowd cheered for the winner.
The Duke of Scone went to help
the knight who lost.

Princess Petunia watched the Duke.

"That is very nice," she thought.

Then the announcer said,

"Next will be the game between

Saturday Knight and Late Knight."

The crowd cheered.

Saturday Knight brushed his hair!

When the Late Knight arrived,

pies flew again!

There was chocolate, banana, apple …

Saturday Knight was creamed!

His hair was a mess!

The Duke helped Saturday Knight.

The Princess watched and smiled.

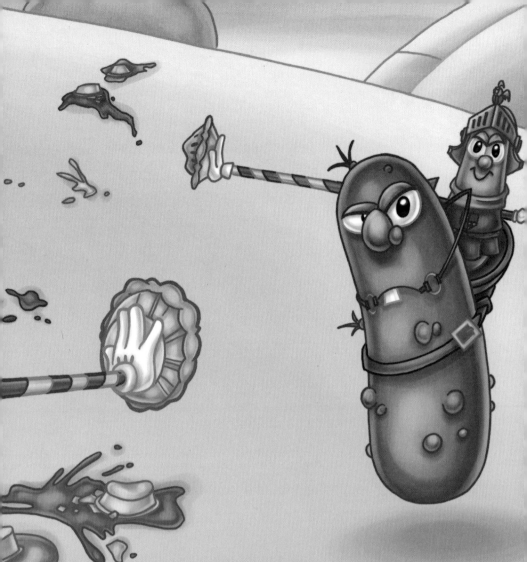

Then, it was the Duke's turn to play.

He had to face the meanest knight of all …

Stormy Knight!

As the two knights took aim,

the Duke heard

a cry from the crowd.

"Mommy!"

The Duke was worried.

He turned to look.

Ka-Pow!

The Duke of Scone was creamed!

But he wasn't sad.

He ran into the seats to

help the lost child.

At the end of the day,

the winner would be named

by one of the fair maidens.

The Queen of Scone tossed some flowers.

Petunia caught them.

SHE would name the big winner!

Petunia walked down to the field.

All the knights were there.

"I choose the Duke of Scone," she said.

"He is the winner!"

All the other knights were mad.

"But Princess," Duke said.

"I lost the pie game!"

"No," said Petunia.

"By helping all the others,

You are a WINNER!"

"Duke of Scone," the queen said,

"for putting others before yourself,

you have won the Great Pie Games!"